# THE BEAR SAYS NORTH

# The Bear Says
# NORTH

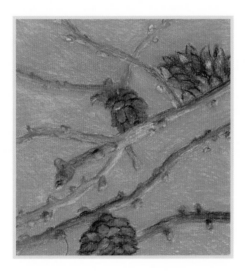

*Tales from Northern Lands*

RETOLD BY

## Bob Barton

ILLUSTRATED BY

## JIRINA MARTON

A GROUNDWOOD BOOK

DOUGLAS & McINTYRE

TORONTO VANCOUVER BERKELEY

Groundwood Books / Douglas & McIntyre
720 Bathurst Street, Suite 500, Toronto, Ontario M5S 2R4

Distributed in the USA by Publishers Group West
1700 Fourth Street, Berkeley, CA 94710

We acknowledge for their financial support of our publishing program the Canada
Council for the Arts, the Ontario Arts Council and the Government of Canada through
the Book Publishing Industry Development Program (BPIDP).

ONTARIO ARTS COUNCIL
CONSEIL DES ARTS DE L'ONTARIO

National Library of Canada Cataloguing in Publication
Barton, Robert
The bear says north: tales from northern lands / by Bob Barton;
illustrated by Jirina Marton.
ISBN 0-88899-533-4
1. Tales–Northern Hemisphere. 2. Tales–Arctic regions.
I. Marton, Jirina  II. Title.
PS8553.A7808B35 2003     j398.2'09181'3     C2002-906142-3
PZ7

Library of Congress Control Number:  2002117070

The illustrations are done in oil pastels on paper.
Book design by Michael Solomon
Printed and bound in China by Everbest Printing Co. Ltd.

In memory of my parents,
Isabelle Irene Wright and Walter Alfred Barton

B B

To Michelle

J M

# CONTENTS

# INTRODUCTION

My INTEREST IN northern tales goes back a long way, beginning with visits to the main branch of the Hamilton Public Library. I was three years old. It was wartime and mother would line up in the foyer of the library to obtain our ration coupons for sugar and butter. Afterwards we would part the heavy velvet drapes that separated the children's section from the adult collections and browse for three books to take home.

Among these early choices, one stands out vividly. It was *Children of the Northern Lights* by Ingri and Edgar Parin d'Aulaire. The images of brightly garbed Lapp children gliding across frozen tundra in sleighs pulled by reindeer or peering with shining faces through clouds of steam in the communal bathhouse are indelible in my mind.

This collection grew out of my fascination with those images and my own firsthand experience of the high Arctic. I don't think I have ever witnessed greater beauty, mystery or harshness. Nor have I ever felt such stillness and silence.

For this collection I have retold stories from northern hemisphere countries that border on or contain frozen tundra, snowy mountains, dense wilderness and ice fields. I have also chosen stories that I think capture something of the beauty, the mystery, the ordinary, the extraordinary, the funny and the serious of the places they are from.

The folktales gathered here have made their way across continents and through centuries by means of oral transmission from one teller to the next. Each person who has told the stories shaped them in his or her own way, adding bits, deleting bits but remaining true to the heart of the tale.

In retelling these stories I have lightly pruned and polished some ("Anders' Hat," "Grandfather Bear" and "How Frog Helped Prairie Wolf Bring Fire to the Humans"). Others such as "The Reindeer Herder and the Moon" have been stripped bare and rebuilt to shape the story to a more satisfying end. Where the atmosphere of a story could benefit from some added detail, I have supplied it ("Good Neighbors" and "Katya and the Goat with the Silver Hoof"). For "The Raven and the Whale" I have drawn on a number of variants recorded over many years from different sources in the western Arctic and retold out of these sources.

The language of folktales is often unusually patterned, with strong rhythms designed to make the tale highly memorable. In "The Honest Penny" I have tried to highlight some of the inherent patterning and draw out the music of the tale.

I have taken the greatest liberties with "The Girl Who Wanted the Northern Lights." The source is *The Stars in the Sky* collected by Joseph Jacobs in the nineteenth century. Jacobs had doubts about the story's authenticity, and in his notes he wrote that the words had been transmitted "through minds tainted with culture and introspection." With this in mind, I did not hesitate to reinvent the story in my own way.

I wish that I had received these tales at the feet of an accomplished oral teller but I didn't. I had to consult books from the nineteenth and early twentieth centuries when many of the stories were collected and rescued from oblivion. When stories cease to live in human minds and imaginations and are no longer passed on to others, they gradually fade away. Despite the popularity of stories such as "Snow White" or "Beauty and the Beast," thousands of others have been forgotten. I believe it is the job of the contemporary storyteller to delve into old sources and find little treasures that can be restored and reintroduced to a new generation of readers and listeners.

It is my wish that readers of this book will find something to surprise, delight and entertain.

Bob Barton
Toronto, 2003

## THE REINDEER HERDER
## AND THE MOON

MOON was lonely.

He had fallen in love with a young reindeer herder on the earth beneath, and he couldn't stop thinking about her.

"Put her out of your mind," warned the stars. "She belongs on earth. Your place is here in the heavens shining along with the rest of us."

But Moon paid no attention. He dreamed of having the girl by his side.

One night, as he watched her returning to her camp on the back of a large reindeer, he was overcome by a powerful urge to fetch her. So he started to climb down.

At first the girl didn't see him. Then she looked up.

"How close the moon appears!" she said.

She raised her hand to shield her eyes from his brightness, and that's when she saw his long spindly legs and skinny arms. The sight of him was terrifying.

"Oh!" she cried. "The Moon Man is coming for me! What can I do?"

Her reindeer turned and spoke.

"Jump from my back. I'll dig a hole in the snow where you can hide."

With his powerful hind legs the reindeer kicked a hollow in

the snow. The girl jumped in and the reindeer pushed snow all around her, leaving only the top of her white fur hood uncovered. Then the reindeer moved into the distance.

Moon stepped onto the earth. His narrow spindly legs felt very strange beneath the weight of his body. He looked from side to side. He had expected to see the herder and her reindeer. He had not expected to see an empty landscape.

"Where is she?" muttered Moon. "She was here only moments ago."

Even as he spoke he was practically standing on top of her. Then he spied reindeer tracks in the snow. He started to follow them, but soon thought better of the idea. He wasn't used to walking about like this.

A heavy feeling came over him. His light had dimmed considerably.

"She's run off," sighed Moon. "I'd better turn back."

With great difficulty, Moon started to climb back into the sky.

The higher he climbed the brighter he became. The higher he climbed the stronger he felt. Soon he floated easily among the stars.

On earth, the reindeer dug the girl from the snow. She leapt onto his back and made haste to her camp.

Suddenly Moon looked down and saw her. This time he didn't climb out of the sky. He plunged instantly toward the earth.

The reindeer saw him coming.

"Moon is returning!" he shouted.

"I must hide!" cried the girl. "Where?"

"I can hide you," said the reindeer. "With my magic powers I can transform you into something else. You could become a tent pole."

"No," said the girl. "He might crush the tent."

"You could become one of the skins on the sleeping platform."

"He could carry that off," replied the girl.

The reindeer looked about hurriedly.

"I have it!" he said. "I can change you into an oil lamp. In the glare of Moon's brightness you will not be seen."

And that's what Reindeer did. He struck his front hoof three times on the surface of the snow, and where the girl had stood there now appeared a stone oil lamp burning with a tiny bright flame.

Reindeer hid as Moon picked his way uncertainly toward the tent.

"Where are you?" he cried. He reached out, lifted the flap and peered in.

"Where are you hiding?" he demanded. "Are you under the sleeping platform?"

He raised the sleeping platform. No one was hiding there.

"Are you behind the tent pole?"

He peeked behind the tent pole. No one was hiding there.

"Are you under the cooking pot?"

He lifted the cooking pot. No one was hiding there.

All the time he looked, the tiny flame fluttered and danced in the Arctic night.

Moon withdrew from the tent. He was baffled.

"How does she disappear like that?" he wondered. "Where does she go?"

There was a giggle from inside the tent.

Moon tore open the tent flap and barged inside. No one was there. Only the tiny lamp flame leapt and whirled in the sudden breeze Moon had made as he entered.

Moon stumbled outside. He did not feel well. A great heaviness had come over him. His light was nearly out.

"The stars were right," thought Moon. "I've no business being down here."

He was about to leave when a peal of laughter rang out! Moon turned. The girl had regained her shape and was peering at him from behind the tent flap.

"Here I am!" she taunted.

Moon lurched toward her, tripped over his feet and crashed to the snow.

The girl was on him in a flash. She threw the reindeer harness around his legs, pulled it tight and shouted, "So, Moon Man, I have captured you."

But Moon said nothing. His teeth chattered violently. His light was almost gone. He appeared completely helpless. When he did speak, his voice came in a whisper.

"Please! Please help me! Unfasten my legs. Let me return to the skies."

"And if I do, you will grow strong again and come chasing after me," said the girl.

"No, never!" cried the moon. "I shall never come down from the skies again. Please release me and I will reward you and all your people."

"And what reward would that be, Moon Man?"

Moon's voice was so weak that the girl had to put her ear right up to his lips to listen. When he finished speaking, her face beamed.

She leapt to her feet, whistled to her reindeer and freed Moon's legs. Then she slipped the harness under Moon's arms and tossed one end to the reindeer. He gripped it in his teeth, and while she pushed from behind, the reindeer pulled.

Slowly, slowly Moon rose to his feet. He put one arm around the girl and the other over the reindeer's back and took a few halting steps. Then he started to climb back into the sky.

Higher and higher he climbed.

Brighter and brighter he became.

Soon Moon had regained his rightful place among the stars.

True to his word, Moon rewarded the girl and her people. He became their nightly beacon, guiding them across the frozen Arctic lands. He became their calendar, measuring the year for them.

> He became for her people
> The Moon of the Old Bull
> The Moon of the Birth of Calves
> The Moon of the Waters.

> He became
> The Moon of Leaves
> The Moon of Warmth
> The Moon of the Shedding of Antlers.

> He became
> The Moon of Love Among the Wild Deer
> The Moon of the First Winter
> The Moon of the Shortening Days.

And true to his word, Moon never came down to earth again.

# THE HONEST PENNY

THERE was once a boy who lived with his mother in the faraway northern lands. They were very poor, and there was often little food for the table or fuel for the fire.

One day the boy was sent out to look for roots and twigs to burn. As he struggled along in the freezing cold, his little fists turned as red as the cranberries that he passed, and he had to run and jump and jump and run to keep himself warm.

When he had gathered all the wood he could carry, he started for home. Suddenly he came upon a large crooked stone that was white with frost.

"Poor old stone," said the boy. "How white and pale you are! Why, I believe you have frozen to death.

The boy threw down his load, took off his jacket and wrapped it around the stone.

When he got home his mother met him at the door.

"What do you think you're doing running about in the middle of winter in your shirt sleeves?" she said.

The boy, all excited, told her about the stone that had turned white and pale from the frost and how he had given it his jacket.

"You featherhead," said his mother, very angry. "Do you really believe that stones can freeze? Even if they could, here's a lesson for you:

> Look to thyself.
> Take care of thyself.
> For nobody cares for thee.

It costs me enough to keep clothes on your back without you leaving them draped on stones. Go back and fetch your jacket!"

The boy returned to the stone but was amazed to discover that it was standing on end. And where the stone had lain there was a box full of silver coins.

"This must be stolen money," thought the boy. "No one puts honest money under a stone."

He picked up the box of coins, took it to a nearby lake and threw it in. As the box sank to the bottom, one silver penny piece floated to the surface.

"Now that," said the boy, "is honest money. What's honest always floats."

He scooped the penny from the lake, put it into the pocket of his jacket and went home.

When his mother heard about the money he had thrown into the lake she burst out crying.

"You're a born fool. If you had kept that money we might have lived well and happily all our days. If nothing but what is honest floats on water there can't be much honesty in the world. Even if the money was stolen ten times over, you found it. I've tried to teach you:

> Look to thyself.
> Take care of thyself.
> For nobody cares for thee.

But are you listening? No! Well, you'll stay no more in my house. Get out and earn your own keep!"

And she pushed the boy out the door and slammed it behind him.

For weeks the boy tramped the country far and long asking for work, but no one would put him to any use.

"You're too small!" said some.

"You're too weak!" said others.

One evening, footsore and bone weary, he found himself outside the house of a wealthy merchant. He went around to the kitchen door and tap-tap-tapped. The cook came out.

"Off you go!" he shouted. "There's no charity here!"

"I need work," said the boy. "I'll fetch water. I'll chop wood. I'll stir the porridge. You don't even have to pay me."

"Mmmm," said the cook. "I could use a kitchen boy. Well, don't stand there gaping. In you come!"

After a time, the merchant called his servants together and announced plans for a trading voyage. Then he asked each and every one of them in turn what he should bring back for them. When it was the kitchen boy's turn to say what he would have, he held out his silver penny.

"What should I buy with this?" laughed the merchant. "There won't be much time lost over this bargain."

"Buy what I can get for it. It's honest money, that I know," said the boy.

The merchant gave his word that he would do his best and put out to sea.

At the first port of call the merchant exchanged fish oil and furs for linseed and barley. At the next he traded for nutmeg and cinnamon. At another he loaded cotton and lace. Each time he dropped anchor, he would get off the ship, go up into town and buy the items his servants had requested.

At last his business was finished and he was about to return home when he put his hand into his pocket and pulled out the kitchen boy's penny.

"Oh, no!" he thought. "I forgot the boy. Must I leave the ship and go all the way into town for the sake of a silver penny?"

Just then an old woman stumbled onto the wharf. She was dragging a sack.

"What have you got in your sack, old mother?" called the merchant.

"Oh, nothing but my grimalkin. I can't afford to feed her any longer. I thought I'd throw her into the sea and good riddance."

Suddenly the merchant had an idea. "Would you take this silver penny for the cat?"

"I would," said the old woman, and she handed him the sack.

The merchant released the cat from the bag. The cat ran straight to the main mast and sat down to lick and groom her coat.

Now, when the merchant had sailed a bit, rough weather fell on them. Thunder crashed, waves lashed, the rain came down in torrents. The ship drove and drove through pounding seas.

At last the merchant was blown onto the shores of a land where he had never set foot before. He went immediately up into town and entered an inn.

A large table was set for a meal, and at each place was a stout stick for the person who sat there.

"This is odd," thought the merchant, and he sat himself down to find out what everyone would do.

By and by others joined him at the table. No sooner had food been served when he saw what the sticks were for. Out from the walls and down from the ceiling beams tumbled hundreds of mice, and each person who sat to eat had to seize a stick and flog and flap about and nothing could be heard but *thwack-thwack-thwack!* Sometimes people accidentally struck each other in the face and barely had time to say beg your pardon before they struck someone else.

"Hard work to eat in this place," cried the merchant.

"Very hard!" shouted the others.

"Have you no cats here?" called the merchant.

"Cats? What are they?" exclaimed the others.

The merchant darted from the inn and fetched the cat he had bought for the kitchen boy. Instantly she ran among the mice, raking them with her claws and scattering them to their hiding places in the walls.

All who ate there agreed that never in living memory had they enjoyed such peace at a meal.

"Sell us that cat," demanded the people. And they gave the merchant a hundred gold coins.

The merchant sailed away again but he had scarcely got good sea room before he discovered that the cat was back, crouched beside the main mast. The merchant grinned at the cat. The cat did not grin back.

Suddenly, foul weather came upon them. Thunder crashed, waves lashed, the rain came down in torrents. The ship drove and drove through heaving seas. When finally the storm died, the merchant found himself on the shores of another land where he had never set foot before.

Immediately he went up to the town and entered an inn. As before a table was set for dinner and at each place there was a stick twice as long and twice as thick as the ones in the inn the night before. And they had to be, for at dinner that evening, the mice that attacked the food were twice as many and twice as large. Attempting to eat took much toil and trouble. Once again the cat was fetched and the mice were banished to their hiding places in the walls. This time the merchant sold the cat for two hundred pieces of gold with no trouble at all.

The merchant had just cleared the harbor when he spied the

cat. It was sitting beside the main mast. The cat narrowed its green eyes and glared at him. The merchant shivered and shook, for he knew what would surely follow.

Suddenly, fearful weather was upon them. Thunder crashed, waves lashed, the rain came down in torrents. The ship drove and drove through rolling seas. When the storm had blown itself out, the merchant found himself on the shores of yet another land where he had never set foot before.

He made his way quickly to the town and into an inn and there was a table set for dinner and the sticks beside each place were as thick as brooms and twice the length of his arm.

When dinner was served that night, rats the size of small dogs swarmed the room. The fighting was so thick that one could scarcely get a morsel into one's mouth.

The merchant scurried from the inn, fetched the kitchen boy's cat and sent it into the fray. In no time at all, the rats were running for their lives.

"We must have that cat!" exclaimed the grateful people.

Before the merchant could say a word, three hundred gold pieces were pressed into his hands and the cat was sold again.

The merchant returned to the ship, weighed anchor and thought happily about all the money he had made out of the kitchen boy's penny.

"Why, this is more money than I've earned on any voyage," he exclaimed.

Suddenly a thought crossed his mind. He frowned. "I suppose I must give the money to the boy." His eyes narrowed. "No, why should I? It's me he has to thank for the cat. And besides, there's an old saying:

> Look to thyself.
> Take care of thyself.
> For nobody cares for thee.

Yes, I'll keep the money."

No sooner had he said this than he felt the hairs rise on the back of his neck. He turned. The cat was back. She was sitting beside the main mast, ears flat, teeth bared, hissing at him.

Suddenly the sea grew angry. The sky grew dark. The terrified merchant cried out, "I'll give all the money to the kitchen boy, I swear it!"

Instantly the sky brightened. A calm fell upon the waves. And the ship was blown home on a snoring breeze.

As he promised, the merchant counted out every gold piece into the boy's hands. The boy was now richer than the merchant, and he and the cat became good friends.

But the story doesn't end here. The boy sent for his mother and shared all of his fortune with her.

"How is this happening?" she asked. "After the way I treated you, how can you do this for me?"

"Because," said the boy, "I never did believe I should look to myself, take care of myself, and that nobody cared for me."

# KATYA AND THE GOAT
# WITH THE SILVER HOOF

WHEN her parents died, Katya moved in with the neighbors next door. She was just six years old.

She arrived at the neighbors' cottage wearing only the clothes she had on and carrying a stray cat she had found along the way.

The neighbors had twelve children of their own. They were not happy about another mouth to feed, and they especially resented the cat eating their food as well. When they tried to get rid of the cat it snarled ferociously and lashed out with its sharp claws.

Other neighbors who pitied Katya went to visit Old Vanka who lived at the edge of the village. "You must take in the child, Vanka. Her life is none too sweet at the moment."

"What can I do for a girl? What can I possibly teach her?" said Old Vanka. But then he thought again. "Maybe the child would bring some joy into the house. But maybe she won't want to live with a lonely old man!"

"Katya may be young but she understands what the family thinks of her. She feels it. She would probably jump at the chance to live with you," the neighbors told him.

The following day Old Vanka paid a visit to Katya. Inside the cottage he was mobbed by a gaggle of gabbling children. Beside the stove, a little girl sat stroking a cat. She looked thin, bedraggled and very unhappy.

Old Vanka nodded to the wife and asked, "Is that the orphan?"

"The same," snapped the wife. "And if it isn't enough that we have to feed her there's the cat on top of it. Mangy beast! Scratches the children. When I tried to get rid of it, it scratched me too!"

Old Vanka knelt down beside Katya. "How would you like to come and live with me?"

"Who are you?" Katya asked.

"Well, I'm a hunter of sorts," said Old Vanka. "In summer I hunt for gold by washing sand from the river bed. In winter I hunt for the goat who lives in the woods, but I never catch sight of him."

"Are you going to shoot him?" asked Katya.

"Oh, no! Not that one, I won't. I want to see where he stamps his front right hoof."

"What for?"

"Why don't you come and live with me and I'll tell you all about it."

Katya was very curious about the goat, and she sensed that Old Vanka was a kind man. "I'll come," she said, "but I must bring my Catonaevich. She's very good, you know."

"I can see that. Only a fool would leave a lovely cat like that behind."

The family gathered Katya's few things together as quickly as they could before the old man changed his mind, and they hurried Katya, Old Vanka and the cat to the door.

So that's how Katya, Catonaevich and Old Vanka came to live together.

Time passed very happily for the three of them. Each day Old Vanka set about his work. Each day Katya played in the cottage, and she taught herself to make soup and porridge. As for Catonaevich, she kept the cottage free of mice.

In the evenings after dinner, Old Vanka told wonderful stories. Katya, all ears, would curl up in a chair with the cat in her lap. But after every story Katya would say, "Now tell me about the goat, Vanka."

At first Old Vanka tried to put her off. Eventually he gave in.

"He's a very special goat, Katya. On his right forefoot he's got a silver hoof. When he stamps that foot he leaves a jewel behind. If he stamps twice there are two, and if he paws the ground he leaves a heap of gems."

The moment the story was out, Old Vanka was sorry he'd ever mentioned the goat. Katya had a mouthful of questions.

"What's his name? Has he got horns? Is he big? Does he bite people? What color is he?"

"Enough, enough! So many questions. Where to begin?" cried Old Vanka. "Well, in summer he's the color of your cat, but in winter his coat turns silver gray. I call him Silver Hoof."

"Does he stink, Vanka?"

"Stink! Heavens, no. Farm goats stink but a wild goat smells of pine bark and bilberries and sweet wild thyme. Now come," said Old Vanka. "It's time you were in bed."

When autumn heaped leaves against the sides of the cottage, Old Vanka stopped looking for gold in the river bed and got ready to go to the woods to see where the wild goats were feeding. Katya pleaded with him to take her along. Old Vanka had to make up excuses to leave her behind.

"There's nothing to see yet, Katya. The goats are too far away."

In the late afternoons when Old Vanka returned, Katya would pester him with questions. "Did you see Silver Hoof, Vanka? How can you tell him from the other goats?"

"Well," said Old Vanka, "Silver Hoof has horns the size of

antlers. You can't miss him even when he's far off." Katya tried to picture Silver Hoof in her mind.

Then one afternoon Old Vanka returned all excited. "Herds of wild goats are feeding about a day's journey from here. When the snows come I will have to move deeper into the woods to get close to them."

"But where will you stay in the woods?" asked Katya.

"I've got a sturdy little hut tucked among the trees," said Old Vanka. "It's not much but there's a window in it and a stove. It's very snug."

"Will Silver Hoof feed with the other goats?" asked Katya.

"He might," said the old man.

"Then I'm coming. Please, Vanka. I won't make any trouble. I'll be very quiet. Maybe Silver Hoof will come close to the hut and I'll see him."

"I can't take you that deep into the woods, Katya. I have to travel on skis and you don't know how. You'd sink into the snow and freeze to death."

"I can learn to ski! Please, Vanka," she begged.

In the end, Old Vanka didn't have the heart to refuse her. "All right," he said. "I'll take you with me, but once we're there you mustn't make a fuss and ask to come home."

When winter's breath became so cold that streams froze and snow wells formed around the boles of the trees, Old Vanka loaded a hand sled with sacks of rusks, pots of honey, tea and hunting supplies. Katya packed her doll, a hank of thread and a needle and some scraps of cloth to make a doll's dress. As an afterthought she included a rope.

"Maybe I can catch Silver Hoof with it," she told herself.

Catonaevich would have to stay behind. Katya stroked her back and talked softly into her ear.

"Old Vanka and I are going to the woods for a few days and you must guard the house against mice. When I see Silver Hoof I promise I'll tell you all about it."

The cat purred and squinted her luminous green eyes as if she were thinking of something else.

At last everything was ready and Old Vanka and Katya set off. They had scarcely got underway when there was a terrible commotion behind them. The village dogs barked and howled as if they had cornered a bear.

Katya and Old Vanka turned. Bounding down the road toward them was Catonaevich, spitting and swearing at the dogs and daring any of them to try to stop her.

Katya ran to catch her but the cat veered sharply, dashed into the woods and clawed her way up a tree. Katya and Old Vanka did everything they could to coax her down, but she wouldn't budge.

"There's nothing for it," said Old Vanka. "We'll have to leave her or we won't get to the hut before dark."

They started off again. Katya turned to say goodbye, but Catonaevich wasn't in the tree. Then Katya saw her. The cat was following them, well off to one side.

So it was that all three of them reached the hut.

Wild goats were plentiful that winter. Each day Old Vanka returned with one or two goats. Each day Old Vanka and Katya salted meat and stacked hides. Then one morning Old Vanka realized that he had far too much to take back on the sled. He'd have to make two trips. But what to do? He couldn't go back and forth with Katya and the cat, but neither could he leave them alone in the woods.

Finally Katya persuaded him that she and the cat would be perfectly fine overnight.

"What is there to be frightened of?" she asked. "I've got

Catonaevich to keep me company and the hut is strong and warm. I won't be scared, but please hurry back."

Old Vanka left reluctantly.

Katya was used to being alone all day when Vanka was out hunting wild goats, but when darkness fell she started to feel uneasy. Catonaevich slept comfortably beside the stove and that made Katya feel better.

She sat down by the window and looked out at the forest. The trees, dressed like snow ghosts, stared solemnly at the little hut.

Suddenly there was a movement at the edge of the clearing. Katya strained her eyes. A goat stepped into the clearing. It had slender legs and a small head crowned with horns the size of antlers. Katya ran to the door and opened it. She found nothing there except the wind whistling a tuneless song as it shook little avalanches of snow from the branches of the trees. She closed the door and snuggled up to the cat.

"I must have been seeing things," said Katya.

Catonaevich stared out the window. Her tail flicked back and forth.

That night thick snow fell. The wind was wild.

All the next day heavy snow leaned on the tall summer grasses, turning them into twisted tunnels where mice and shrews and gophers and moles played their deadly game of hide-and-seek. Katya felt very lonely. She stroked the cat.

"Don't worry, cat," she said. "Old Vanka will get here tomorrow."

"Miaou," the cat answered.

That evening, Katya looked out at the snowbound forest. Suddenly she jumped up. The goat with the big horns was standing quite close to the hut. Katya ran to the door, opened it and peeped out. She looked at the goat. The goat looked at Katya and raised his front forefoot. A silver hoof flashed. The goat *maaaed* and sprang into the trees.

Katya closed the door and picked up the cat. "I've seen him! I've seen Silver Hoof!" she cried. "I saw his horns and his hoof but I didn't see him stamp and leave precious stones. He'll do that next time. I know he will."

The cat arched her back. Her tail thrashed back and forth.

A third day came and still Old Vanka did not appear. Katya's face was glum. Tears gathered in the corners of her eyes.

As darkness fell, Katya needed to cuddle with Catonaevich. The cat was nowhere to be found. Now Katya was really frightened. She pulled on her coat and boots and ran outside to look for her.

It was a full-moon night. Trees cast long narrow shadows over the cold white snow. And sitting among the shadows was Catonaevich, staring into the eyes of Silver Hoof the goat. Both animals were nodding their heads as if they were having a chat.

Then they began to chase each other backward, forward and around and around. Each time the goat paused, it stamped its silver hoof. Precious stones flashed out of the snow like sparks at first, and then they gleamed pink and blue and green and violet.

It was at that moment that Old Vanka returned. He couldn't believe the beautiful colors sparkling and winking in the snow. He stared at the cat and the goat as they cavorted all over the clearing.

Old Vanka leaned over to scoop up some of the precious stones but Katya begged him not to touch them.

"Please, Vanka. Leave them. I want to look at them like this all night."

Sometime during the night, Katya and Old Vanka fell asleep at the window. While they slept the wind lifted the heavy blanket of snow and whirled it around in eddies.

In the morning Katya and Old Vanka hurried outside and searched the snowdrifts. The jewels were gone. Silver Hoof was gone. Catonaevich was gone, too.

So it all ended. It was a shame about Catonaevich. She was never seen again. Silver Hoof didn't come back, either.

But he had come once. And that was enough to occupy the dreams of Katya and Old Vanka for the rest of their lives.

# FROSTBITE

"BRAGGART!" spluttered Old Frost. "Wild thing! Headstrong, that's what he is."

He watched as his son, Young Frost, ran toward a horse and sleigh coming along the road.

"Thinks I'm too old and too weak to freeze people," continued Old Frost to himself. "Thinks he can lick anyone he pleases."

By now Young Frost had reached the road. A sleek young horse pranced proudly in front of a sleigh driven by a plump, prosperous-looking fellow. As the sleigh passed, Young Frost jumped onto a back runner and looked the man over.

The man wore a brown bearskin coat, its collar pulled up well over his ears. A furry hat was pressed down over his forehead, and his legs were swaddled in a warm woolen rug.

Young Frost rubbed his hands in anticipation of what was to follow. "Father wouldn't be able to freeze you," he thought, "but I'll turn your marrow to ice."

With that, Young Frost let out a "Whoop!" and descended on the man in a swirl of icy mist. He nipped the man's cheeks, he tweaked his nose, he dove into his leather boots and froze his toes. He breathed down his collar and pinched his ears so hard the man was brought to tears.

The man was now shivering so much that he nearly slid off the

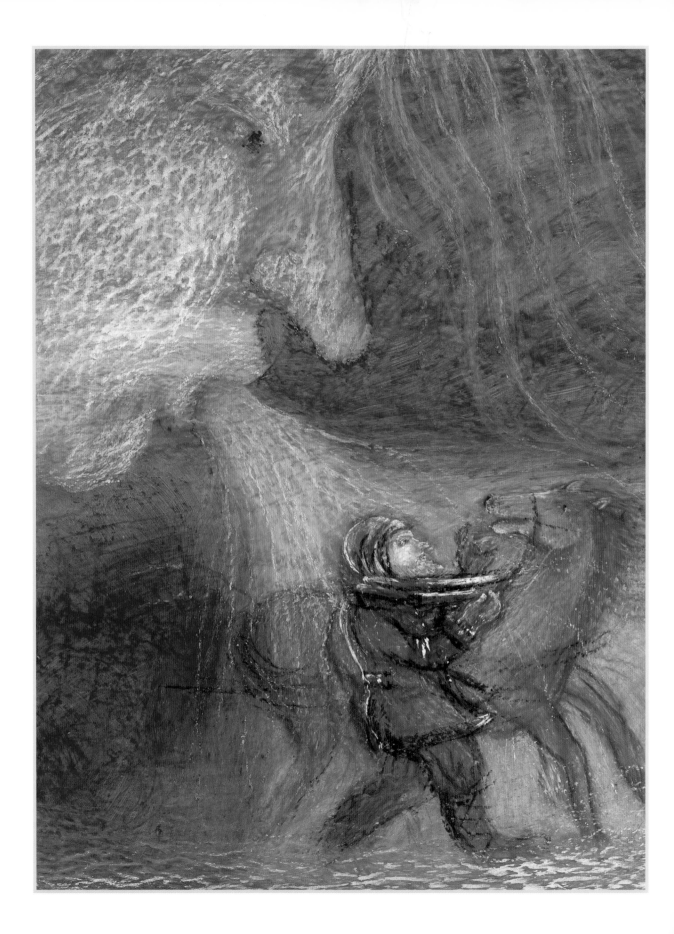

seat. He tried twisting the blanket more tightly around his legs and scrunched down inside his collar, but the shivering wouldn't stop. He cracked the whip and the horse broke into a gallop.

Young Frost slipped his icy fingers around the man's throat and began to squeeze. The man felt his face growing stiff. He cracked the whip again and tried to cry out to the horse, but his breath froze in his throat. A sudden bend in the road caused the horse to turn so sharply that the sleigh tipped up on one runner. Young Frost lost his grip and was hurled into a snowdrift.

Foaming and sweating, the horse galloped up to the man's front door. Servants rushed out and half carried him into the house, where his ice-solid clothing was peeled off, his feet plunged into a basin of warm water and his body thawed with cups of hot tea.

Young Frost dusted the snow from his robe and swaggered back to his father.

"Did you see that, Father? Did you see how quickly I put the chill on him? If the sleigh hadn't swerved so suddenly I'd have turned him into a block of ice!"

"It was hardly a fair fight now, was it?" snorted Old Frost. "The man had no idea how to protect himself. If you want to show me what a wonder you are, try to freeze that poor peasant over there."

Young Frost looked in the direction his father was pointing. A rickety-looking horse plodded toward them dragging a broken-down sledge that was held together with lengths of fraying rope. The driver, a poor woodcutter, was dressed in a shabby, thread-bare coat. A tattered woolen muffler was tied around his head. There were holes in his mittens, and he had stuffed his cloth boots with straw to keep his feet warm.

"He's on his way to cut firewood," said Old Frost. "If you can freeze him, then I'll really believe that you are as strong and powerful as you say you are."

"Not much of a test for my skills," sneered Young Frost. "Stay right where you are, Father. I'll freeze him before you can say Jack Frost." And Young Frost went after the peasant in leaps and bounds. He took no time to look over his prey but fell onto the peasant's neck and breathed hard down his collar. The peasant shuddered. Young Frost clenched his icy fists and jabbed at the worn parts of the coat close to the man's ribs. The peasant beat his arms against his sides and kept going.

Young Frost zipped into the peasant's boots. He tried to nip his toes but got a mouthful of straw instead. The peasant jumped off the sledge, grasped the halter and began to jog beside the horse.

"Hey, what do you think you're doing?" cried Young Frost, very annoyed.

By now the peasant had reached the forest. He took his ax from the sledge and began to chop down a tree. The ax bit so hard into the frozen tree bark that sparks flew in all directions.

Young Frost jumped back in terror. This rude fellow was putting him in a terrible temper. Young Frost gnawed the bare flesh that showed through the peasant's tattered mittens. He dug his icicle-sharp fingernails into every hole in the man's coat. But the harder Young Frost tried to freeze him, the faster and harder the peasant chopped.

Then the peasant performed an unspeakable act. He threw down his ax, shook off his mittens and tore the woolen muffler from his head. When Young Frost saw steam rising from the man's damp hair, he nearly lost heart.

"If I can't get you now," said Young Frost to himself, "I'll get you on the way back." And he crept over to the man's mittens. He breathed into one until it was as hard as a rock. Then he crawled into the other, froze it and waited.

When the peasant had chopped enough wood to fill the sledge, he picked up his mittens and tried to put them on. But the mittens were so hard and stiff that he couldn't squeeze his hands into them.

The peasant had an idea. He picked up his ax and began hammering his gloves with the blunt end. *Wank, wank, wank* went the ax.

"Ooh, ow, oh," cried Young Frost from inside one of the gloves.

Old Frost watched the thrashing his son was getting and laughed so hard that he had to hold onto his sides.

Between blows, Young Frost managed to break free. He staggered back to his father. His feet felt like lead and his ribs ached.

"Ha!" said Old Frost. "Bit of bad luck there, son." And he stroked his chin to hide a smile. "What are you going to try next?"

"Of all the spiteful, mule-headed, fish-faced geezers. I couldn't freeze him," groaned Young Frost. "I'm going home. Oh, my aching sides!"

"You must realize," said Old Frost, "that unlike the first unfortunate fellow, the peasant is used to a hard and hearty outdoor life. He knows you have to keep moving to avoid freezing. But cheer up. All is not lost. There's a market in the village today. Why don't we go over there and worry a few old people and some small children?"

Old Frost started off in the direction of the village. Young Frost straggled along behind, kicking snow in all directions as hard as he could.

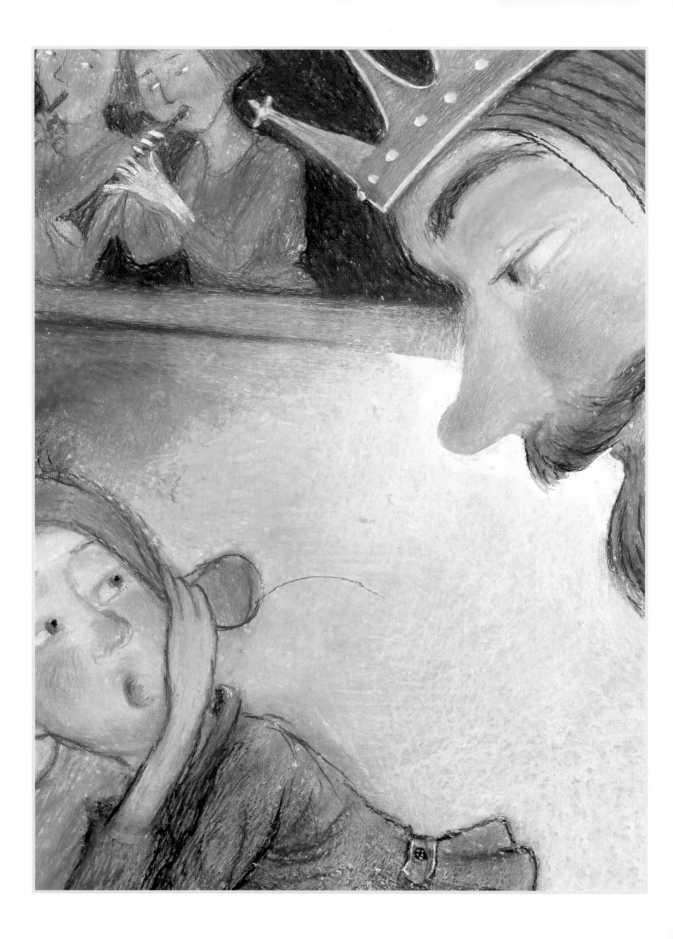

# ANDERS' HAT

THERE was once a little boy named Anders who had a new hat. His mother had knit it for him and a finer hat was not to be found – not even in the shops.

It was mostly red except for a wee bit in the middle that was green, for the red yarn had run out. The tassel was blue.

Anders' brothers and sisters gathered around him gazing and gazing at the hat.

"Nobody makes anything quite as nice as Mother," they said.

"I'm going out now to show it off," Anders said, and he pulled the hat down over his ears, stuffed his hands into his trouser pockets and strode proudly down the road. Flowers growing along the roadside nodded gently as Anders passed.

The first person he met was a woodcutter sitting on the trunk of a pine tree. The man pulled off his leather cap and bowed so low that his nose nearly touched the ground.

"Dear me," he said, raising his eyebrows. "I was sure it was the young prince himself wearing that fine hat. Look here, will you swap it for mine? I'll pay good money."

"Oh, no!" said Anders, shaking his head and hurrying away. "This is the hat my mother made."

The next person Anders met was a large boy with a hank of hair falling across his face. He was whittling a piece of wood with a jackknife.

"Whoa!" he said to Anders. "Let's see the hat." And he walked around Anders and flicked the blue tassel with his thumb and forefinger.

"I'll trade this knife for your hat," said the boy, holding up the blade.

Now the knife was a beautiful one, even if the tip of the blade was broken off and the ivory handle was chipped. And Anders knew that owning a jackknife was a sign of being practically a grown-up.

But he was not that easily fooled. The knife simply wasn't good enough.

"No trade," he cried. "This is the hat that Mother made." And he hurried along as the boy made faces at him because he couldn't have the hat.

Up ahead, Anders could see an old woman leading a white horse hitched to a brightly painted wagon. As they drew close, the woman turned to look at Anders. Her long red skirt swished over the toes of her boots.

"Good day, young man," she called out. "Are you off to the ball at the royal court with that hat?"

"Well," thought Anders, "why not? My hat is getting so much attention I may as well show it to the king."

And that's just what he did.

At the palace gates, two guards in shining helmets stood as stiff as the halberds they clutched in their hands. Anders tried to walk between them but they crossed their halberds to stop him.

"Halt!" shouted one of the guards. "Where do you think you're going?"

"I'm going to the royal ball," answered Anders.

"I don't think so," said the other guard. "This is a fancy dress ball. No one gets in without a smart outfit."

The princess, who was playing in the courtyard, overheard the guards. She walked over to Anders.

"Oh," she said, "he is wearing a splendid hat on his head. That counts as fancy dress." And she hurried Anders into the palace.

Anders couldn't believe his eyes. They walked up broad marble stairs where guards stood at attention on every other step. They passed through magnificent halls lit by hundreds of candles in gold chandeliers. Servants dressed in velvet and silk bowed wherever they went.

"They must think I look like a prince in my new hat," thought Anders.

At the farthest end of the largest hall, tables stood in long rows. They were covered in tablecloths of royal blue and set with silver plates and goblets. There were platters of fresh fruit, creamy cakes and side dishes of chocolate and candied fruit. Anders had never seen anything so lovely.

The princess escorted Anders to some gold chairs that had been placed in front of scarlet banners. Overhead hung garlands of yellow roses. She sat in one of the chairs and invited Anders to sit beside her.

The princess leaned over to Anders and whispered, "You must not eat with your hat on. Remove it at once."

"Oh, yes, I can eat just as well with it on," said Anders, and he held onto his hat with both hands. Besides, he thought, if he took it off, no one would think he was a prince. And he might not get the hat back.

"If you give it to me," teased the princess, "I will give you a kiss."

Now the princess was lovely. Anders was bewitched by her beauty. He would have dearly liked to be kissed by her, but he was not about to give up the hat his mother had made on any condition.

He shook his head. No.

"Not even now?" said the princess, and she stuffed his pockets with chocolates and candies wrapped in shiny paper. Then she slipped her diamond necklace over his head, leaned over and kissed him on the cheek.

Anders squirmed in his chair and clapped his hands tightly to his hat.

Suddenly trumpets sounded, doors were thrown open and the king entered at the head of a large party of guests. They were dressed in glittering gowns, bright uniforms and plumed hats. The king wore a purple cape trimmed with ermine. On his head was a large golden crown.

He smiled when he saw Anders sitting in the royal chair.

"That's a fine hat you are wearing," he said.

"Yes, it is," said Anders. "Mother knit it herself of the best yarn, and everyone wants me to give it away."

"Would you exchange hats with me?" asked the king. "My crown for your woolly hat?" And he lifted the gleaming crown from his head.

Anders did not answer. He sat holding onto the hat that everybody seemed to want.

But as the king came closer, holding the crown in his outstretched arms, a thought crossed Anders' mind. "Kings can do what they like, and this king is likely to take the hat that Mother made anyway."

At that moment, Anders was more frightened than he had ever been in his life. He slid to the floor, crawled under the table and bolted past the startled king. He ran as fast as he could, twisting and turning through the outstretched arms of guests, guards and servants.

As he pelted down the stairs two at a time, the princess's diamond necklace fell off his neck. Chocolates and candies popped out of his pockets.

But he had his hat. He held onto it with both hands. At the gate the guards lowered their halberds, and Anders darted around them like a terrified rabbit.

He was still holding onto his hat as he dashed inside his cottage.

His mother scooped him up onto her lap and Anders, breathing hard and sobbing, told her about his adventure and how everybody wanted his hat. His brothers and sisters listened with mouths agape.

But when he came to the part about how he had refused the king's crown for his hat, his big brother frowned. "You refused a king's crown. How could you! Just imagine all the fine things we could have had in exchange for a gold crown. Why, you could have had a finer hat."

Anders felt terrible. His face grew hot. He hadn't thought about that.

"Mother, did I do the wrong thing?"

His mother held him close.

"No, my little one," she said gently. "If you were dressed in a king's gold and silk robes from the top of your head to the tip of your toes, you would not look nicer than you do in your red woolly hat."

Anders snuggled close to his mother. He felt brave again, for he knew well enough that the hat his mother had made was the best hat in the world.

# GOOD NEIGHBORS

THERE was once a woman named Matte and a man named Toller, and they moved into a tumbledown cottage at the mouth of a wild heathland. From that moment on their friends stopped coming to visit.

"There are trolls living out there. Fierce mountain trolls!" they exclaimed. "What are you thinking?"

But trolls didn't frighten Matte and Toller.

"If you do what is fair and right to all living things, there's nothing to be afraid of," they explained.

Nevertheless, their friends stayed away. They were much too terrified.

Matte and Toller worked hard. They hammered, sawed, plastered and painted. They mended the broken windows, fixed the sagging moss-covered roof and replaced doors. In no time the little cottage was cozy and snug.

Now it happened that one evening as Matte and Toller were climbing into bed there was a loud *thump, thump, thump* on the door.

Toller glanced nervously at Matte. Together they tiptoed to the door and opened it a crack.

Suddenly the door was pushed wide and a little man brushed past the startled couple.

"Good evening," he cried in a shrill voice.

He wore a red cap on his head. His white beard touched the floor. Tied around his waist was a leather apron that held a hammer, a chisel and tongs.

Matte and Toller knew instantly that he was a troll, but he appeared friendly and good natured and they were not afraid of him.

"Well, I see," said the little fellow, looking at them with sharp, bright eyes, "that you know well enough who I am."

"We do!"

"Do you intend to live here?"

"Most certainly."

"Then let me explain how matters stand," said the little man. "We are poor mountain trolls whom people have left no other homes on earth save deep caves where the sun can never shine down upon us. Our king fears that you might harm us and he sends me to beg you to let us live in peace."

"Stars above!" cried Matte. "Toller and I would never harm a fly. The world is plenty big enough for all of us."

"Excellent! Excellent!" replied the troll. And he nearly jumped out of his skin with joy. "In return," he promised, "we will do you all the good in our power. Now, good-night."

As he skipped toward the open doorway, Matte called, "Will you not take a bite of supper?" And she rushed to the stove and spooned porridge into a bowl.

"Thank you, no," called the troll. "Our king awaits my return. I must deliver this good news immediately."

And with that the little fellow vanished into the night.

In the weeks and months that followed, Matte and Toller toiled in their fields – clearing rocks, tilling, planting and weeding. From time to time they caught a glimpse of the trolls going in and out of their caves. Always they were careful to do nothing to disturb them.

The trolls soon lost their fear of the couple and went in and out of their cottage as if it were their own. If they borrowed a pot or copper kettle from the kitchen, they always brought it back again and set it on the same spot from which they had taken it.

In return, they repaid Toller and Matte with many kindnesses. Sometimes they would come out of their caves during the night, break stones, gather them from the fields and heap them along the edges. At harvest time they collected fallen ears of corn from the fields and stacked them neatly beside the cottage so that none were lost to the couple.

Each holiday season Toller and Matte set out in front of the caves nice dishes of fine milk porridge.

Time went on and one day Matte gave birth to a baby girl. They named the child Inge. Shortly afterwards Matte became so ill that Toller feared for her life. He went from farm to farm, village to village, henwife to pastureman, alehouse to apothecary seeking advice, but no one knew what to suggest to make her well again.

Night after night Toller stayed up to comfort Matte and look after the baby. One night he was so tired that he fell asleep on his feet. Suddenly he woke with a start. The cottage teemed with trolls. There were trolls scrubbing floors. There were trolls washing dishes. The cottage looked as fresh and as clean as a spring morning. Then Toller noticed a troll rocking Inge and another beside Matte's pillow holding a special herb potion to her lips.

As soon as the trolls discovered that Toller was watching, they cleared out of the cottage like a herd of stampeding sheep. The following morning Matte seemed better. Before many days had passed she was able to leave her bed and take up her work again.

And so it went over many years that Matte, Inge, Toller and the trolls lived in peace and harmony. With each passing year the family's situation grew better. Eventually the little cottage was replaced by a roomier house, the cramped shed by an airy barn and the barren wild heath became a patchwork of copper-colored wheat fields, beds of yellow sunflowers, rows of silk tasseled corn and lush green pastures.

Then one evening as Toller and Matte settled into bed there was a *thump*, *thump*, *thump* at the door, and the little troll entered.

Toller and Matte sat up in surprise. He was not in his usual outfit. On his head he wore a shabby woolen cap. A heavy muffler was wrapped around his neck. A sheepskin was draped over his shoulders. His cheeks were stained with tears.

"Greetings to you both," he sniffed. "Our king has requested that you all come with me now to our mountain. It is a matter of great importance."

More tears ran down the side of the man's nose as he said this. Toller and Matte tried to comfort him and learn the reason for his sadness, but the little fellow only wept more and would not tell them about the cause of his grief.

Matte, Toller and Inge followed him outside into the damp mist. They crossed the grazing pastures and tramped through brush and bramble. They entered a narrow valley and stumbled over sharp ragged rocks. Gradually the ground sloped down and they entered the mouth of a soaring granite cave decorated with huge bunches of sweet willow, cotton grass, crowfoot and other wildflowers that once grew on the heath. At the far end a long table stretched across the width of the cave. It was lit with candles and heaped with wortbread, ham sausage, rye cake, speckled apples and thick wedges of yellow cheese. A horde of trolls crowded around the table with their heads down. Nobody spoke.

Nobody moved. The family was squeezed in next to the troll king. Then the trolls began to eat gloomily and there was much sighing, coughing and rubbing of eyes.

Something was terribly wrong.

When the meal was over, the troll king rose to his feet. "Toller, Matte and Inge, I invited you here to express our goodwill and thank you for the kindness you have shown us over the many years we have been neighbors. But now we are forced to flee. This once wild heath has given way to too many new farms and too many people. The smell of bacon frying, the noise of church bells ringing, ringing, ringing, and the barking of dogs is more than we can bear. Once again we must seek new homes in the wild forests to the north. And so we bid you farewell."

When the troll king had finished speaking, all the trolls came to Matte and Toller and shook hands with them. But when they came to Inge they said, "To you dear Inge we give something to remember us by when we have gone."

As they said this each took up a stone from the ground and dropped it into the pocket of Inge's apron. Then one by one they filed out of the cave, each carrying a backpack and clutching a stout walking stick, as their king led the way.

Matte, Inge and Toller followed them outside. They stood squinting their eyes to hold back the tears. Then, feeling more lonely than they had ever felt in their lives, they made their way back across the heath.

When she woke the next morning, Inge remembered the stones in her apron pocket. She emptied them onto her bed. She couldn't believe her eyes. The stones were all a-dazzle! They shone and sparkled emerald, amethyst, cobalt, jet, sapphire and silver gray.

Inge called out to her mother and father.

"Look," she said, holding out a handful of stones. They all marveled at the shiny blues, blacks, greens, grays and ambers.

"Oh, Inge," cried her mother. "Do you know what this is? The trolls have given the colors of their eyes to the stones. That's what they have left you to remember them by."

And to this day precious stones sparkle and shine because the mountain trolls gave them the colors of their eyes, so that Inge, Matte and Toller would never forget them.

# GRANDFATHER BEAR

GRANDFATHER Bear padded softly through the trees as he made his way to the edge of the lake. His mind was supposed to be on hunting for food, but he couldn't stop thinking about his troubles.

"Everyone's laughing behind my back," he fumed. "The chipmunks make fun of my fishing. Even when I make my catch they say it's not much for a large appetite."

Sadly it was true. The old bear was much slower these days. There were many occasions on which he returned to his lair with an empty belly. His once glossy coat had lost its shine, and it hung from his bones like a tarpaulin tossed over a bale of hay.

Bear emerged from the trees and stepped onto the stony beach. He rose up on his haunches, pointed his nose high in the air and sniffed.

At that moment a low-flying gull swerved to miss him, struck a tree and plummeted to the ground.

Grandfather Bear lost no time snatching the gull in his teeth, then stood up to display his prize to any who might be watching.

He turned slowly back into the woods and made a long detour to his lair. He was in no hurry. He wanted as many woodland creatures as possible to see him. He paused frequently to rise up and turn around so that no one could miss him.

It was while he was making a grand posture that Fox came

upon him. Fox saw the gull in Grandfather Bear's mouth but pretended not to notice.

"I was wondering," he said, gazing up at the sky, "from which direction the wind is blowing."

Now, Grandfather Bear might have been a bit slow, but he wasn't completely stupid. He knew Fox was trying to trick him into opening his mouth so that he would have to let go of the gull. He turned his back and said nothing.

"That's odd," said Fox. "I remember a time, Grandfather Bear, when you'd have been able to answer that question without having to think about it. Why, I even remember when you were wise enough to explain from what direction the wind is blowing when the noonday sun shines in your eyes and you feel the wind tickle your back. But I guess those days are long past."

This was too much for Grandfather Bear. If there was one thing he prided himself on, it was his knowledge of wind and weather.

"From the north!" he roared. But when he said it his mouth opened and the gull fell out.

Fox snapped it up in his teeth, turned tail and sped away.

Grandfather Bear heaved a sigh and shambled back to his lair, too disgusted with himself to hunt any more that day.

# THE LITTLE GIRL WHO WANTED
# THE NORTHERN LIGHTS

In a village in the far north there once lived a girl who wanted to play with the Northern Lights in the sky. She wanted them so badly, she cried for them from morning until night. One day she set out to see if she could find them.

She ran, one foot lifting her and the other setting her down. She ran as fleet-footed as the hare until she came to a mill wheel creaking and grinding away.

"Good day to you," said the girl. "I want the Northern Lights to play with. Have you seen them near here?"

"Ah, yes," said the mill wheel. "Every night they visit my pond and shine in my face until I cannot sleep. Jump into the pond and you will find them."

So the girl jumped into the pond and swam about, but she couldn't find the Northern Lights. She climbed out of the pond and ran some more, one foot lifting her, the other setting her down. She ran as nimble-footed as the ground squirrel until she came to a stream.

"Good day to you," said the girl. "I want the Northern Lights to play with. Have you seen them near here?"

"Ah, yes," said the stream. "They gleam and glimmer on my banks all night until I cannot sleep. Paddle about in my waters and you will find them."

So the girl paddled about in the stream but she couldn't find the Northern Lights. She climbed out and ran on, one foot lifting her, the other setting her down. She ran as light-footed as the stoat.

When it came night she entered a forest. Now this was a magic place where Cailleach Bheur,* the blue-faced hag of winter, gathered her herds of wild deer.

"Good evening to you," said the girl. "I want the Northern Lights to play with. Have you seen them near here?"

"Ah, yes," said Cailleach Bheur, hovering over her. "They dance over my head all night until I cannot sleep. Come with me and you will find them."

All night the girl followed the winter spirit. All night Cailleach Bheur touched the autumn leaves with her staff, causing them to drop from the trees. But they did not find the Northern Lights.

When it came morning, Cailleach Bheur hurried back to her herds.

"Ask Longlegs to carry you to Silversides, she called as she left. "Ask Silversides to take you to Blizzard's Lodge. Cross the great bridge of ice and you will find the Northern Lights."

The girl thought this all very strange. She wandered this way and that way, not knowing which way to go when suddenly she came upon an elk with great spreading antlers.

"Good day, Longlegs," said the girl. "Will you carry me to Silversides?"

"I wait for Cailleach Bheur's bidding," said Longlegs.

"It is from Cailleach Bheur that I come," said the child.

"Then jump on my back," said Longlegs, and they sprang away in leaps and bounds through forests, over mountains and tundra until at last they came to the shores of a great northern sea.

*Pronounced *Cal-yach vare*.

"I can take you no farther," said Longlegs.

The girl looked out over the sea. In the middle distance she glimpsed a world of frost and ice. Snow lay in whirling drifts, forests of icicles hung from giant pans of ice. Rising out of the ice pans was a huge lodge formed of frozen snow.

A large silver fish swam from under the ice pans and up to the girl.

"Good day, Silversides," said the girl. "I want the Northern Lights to play with. Will you carry me to Blizzard's Lodge so that I can see them?"

"I wait for Cailleach Bheur's bidding," said Silversides.

"It is from Cailleach Bheur that I come," said the girl.

"Then jump on my back," said Silversides.

So Silversides swam and swam with the girl on his back until they reached an ice bridge that led to the snowy lodge.

"I can take you no farther," said Silversides.

So the girl jumped from Silversides' back and crossed the ice bridge. She parted the hides covering the entrance of the lodge and stepped into a great hall. The roof was supported by towering pillars of blue ice. Burning oil in stone lamps gave off a pale golden glow but no heat. Sleeping platforms lined the walls, and heaped on them were the skins of the northern white bear.

Suddenly the girl heard the *crunch, crunch* of heavy feet and the boisterous voices of men outside. She parted the hides and peeped out.

Seven shining young warriors trooped onto the ice bridge. They wore painted hide breastplates and carried bronze shields.

They swung clubs made from the jawbone of the narwhal and amid much laughter and shouting they rained blows on one another's shields until the night sky was filled with ribbons of shimmering blue, pink, green and violet light.

"The Northern Lights," breathed the girl.

When the warriors tired of their mock battle, they started toward the lodge. The girl burrowed quickly under the skins on the sleeping platform.

The warriors entered the lodge, threw down their clubs and shields and feasted, laughed, drank and told stories until their heads slumped to their chests and they slept soundly.

The girl crawled out from under the skins and drifted among the sleeping warriors as lightly as a feather. She drew her fingers over the scuff marks on the beautiful bronze shields. Then she began to rub and polish the shields with the edge of her sleeve until the scuff marks disappeared and the shields gleamed in the pale light of the dancing lamp flames.

She had scarcely finished her work when the warriors began to stir. She dove under the hides just as one of the warriors sat up.

"Brothers!" he cried. "Wake up. Here is something curious."

The others jumped to their feet. They marveled at the beautifully polished shields and looked about, puzzled.

"Dawn," cried one of the warriors. "We must be off."

A narrow band of light had begun to separate the darkness from the land. One by one the warriors scooped up their shields and clubs and darted outside. They leapt over dawn's yawning chasm of light and sprinted into the receding dark.

The girl stepped outside. At that moment the ice witch, Blizzard, gusted over the ice fields, driving black clouds ahead and trailing thick sleet behind.

The girl scurried over the ice bridge, one foot lifting her and the other setting her down. She ran as speedily as the lemming to the edge of the ice pans.

Silversides swam toward her and she jumped onto his back.

Silversides took her back to the shore where Longlegs stood

waiting. The girl thanked Silversides and jumped onto Longlegs' back. Longlegs carried her over tundra, mountains and into the forest where their journey had begun. The girl thanked Longlegs, then ran home to her mother, one foot lifting her, the other setting her down. She ran as surely as the fox.

She had found the Northern Lights and she never cried for them again.

# HOW FROG HELPED PRAIRIE WOLF
## BRING FIRE TO THE HUMANS

To BEGIN WITH, Frog had a long, green, glistery tail.

"Oooh, it's sooo lovely!" cooed all of Frog's swampy admirers.

Then one day Prairie Wolf asked Frog for a favor, and that changed everything.

In those days the humans had no fire. All the fire in the world belonged to two terrifying hags who kept it in their lodge and guarded it jealously.

Each evening when the sun's red ball stepped behind the mountains, the humans gazed at it and wished they might catch just one spark to warm themselves.

During the long, cold winter nights when the wind shivered their bones and cut them sharply with needles of ice, the people huddled under their bearskin robes and longed for the precious fire.

Many times they had gone to the hags to try to obtain fire. They had begged for it, offered to barter for it and, I'm sorry to say, they had even tried to steal it.

Finally they decided to ask the animals to help them. But who should they ask?

Some suggested they ask Bear.

"He's very clumsy. And besides, he growls too much," complained others.

Some wanted to ask Elk.

"Too tall! Those antlers would get caught in the lodge poles," said others.

When it came to Snake, everyone voted him down.

"Can't be trusted," they all agreed.

The humans sat for ever so long arguing about this animal and that animal until someone suggested Prairie Wolf.

"He's always hungry. If we offer some food he might agree to help."

So the humans went in search of Prairie Wolf. They found him sniffing at the ground trying to locate a hunter's trail where he might find some leftovers – a bit of meat that had been dropped or a bone to crack and suck.

Prairie Wolf rested his nose on his paws and listened as the humans explained their errand. He felt flattered but he was much too cunning to show it. At first he pretended not to be interested, but when they gave him gifts of buffalo steaks and bear ham, he could no longer hide his pleasure.

"I'll do it," he barked.

That night, Prairie Wolf curled himself up tight, put his nose under his paws, whisked his tail about his feet and thought deep within himself.

"I must have a good plan."

In the morning he set out to recruit other animals to help him. This was a job he could not do alone.

The small animals did not dare refuse him. The larger ones took pity on him.

"Poor old bag of bones. We'd better help."

Frog, who had never been asked to participate before, was very excited.

Prairie Wolf gathered his team together and put his plan into action.

One of the humans was instructed to hide behind a rock close to the lodge where the hags lived. The others were placed at certain distances according to their strength and the challenges of the landscape.

First was Cougar. He sat looking nervous, twitching his ears and tail. Next came Bear, who fussed about, rubbing his back up and down against the rough bark of a tree.

Bat was snugly fastened to a tree branch in her assigned place. Farther along, Squirrel perched hesitantly on a rock. Her tail trembled violently.

Frog, swollen with excitement, was placed just across the lake from the camp of the humans.

Prairie Wolf threw himself into the icy waters of the lake, then approached the lodge of the hags dripping and shivering, and scratched at the door with his paws.

The hags laughed out loud at the sight of him.

"Poor miserable Prairie Wolf," they said, unafraid. "Come in and warm yourself by the fire."

Prairie Wolf limped to the center of the lodge and flopped down beside the fire. He closed his eyes and pretended to sleep. The hags dozed comfortably beside him. The lodge was silent.

Suddenly Prairie Wolf signaled his team with two sharp barks. The hags took this to mean that Prairie Wolf was pleased by the warmth. They nodded approvingly.

All at once there was a fearful clatter. Rocks were being hurled at the side of the lodge by the human. The hags ran outside to investigate. Prairie Wolf seized a flaming brand between his teeth and in a flash slipped past the hags. He ran and ran and ran with the hags wailing, howling and screeching after him in full pursuit.

"He tricked us. After the trickster!"

So terrifying were their thin, high-pitched voices that Prairie Wolf ran all the faster.

"Oh, my poor feet," he moaned. He was not used to running this hard. Just as he thought his legs would collapse, he passed the brand to Cougar, who bounded away through the trees. Cougar was very fast, and by the time the flaming brand was passed on to Bear, the hags had fallen far behind.

Bear was so excited he couldn't stop growling. Each time he growled his jaws opened, and he dropped the brand and had to turn around to pick it up. The hags were gaining on him very quickly. Just as one of them reached out to grab him, Bat swooped down, seized the brand and climbed high, high into the sky.

Bat led the hags a merry chase over the treetops, in and out of canyons and behind waterfalls. She dodged and circled and changed directions, sometimes flying high above them and some-times flying between their heads. By the time she tossed the brand to Squirrel, the hags' tongues were dangling from the sides of their mouths.

Squirrel, unfortunately, had trouble. The brand had burned so short that the heat scorched her cheeks. As she leapt from tree branch to tree branch showers of sparks singed her tail so severely that it curled up over her back, and it has stayed that way ever since. But Squirrel was brave and plunged on.

The hags took heart when they saw Squirrel's difficulty. They gathered their skirts about them and whooshed along even faster.

"We've got you now!" they screamed.

Just in time, Squirrel reached Frog and dropped the tiny flaming brand. Frog opened his mouth wide, caught the little piece and started to hop furiously. But the smoke blinded his eyes, and he was choking so hard that the hags got close enough to swat his tail with their bony hands.

They were just about to snatch him when Frog reached the lake, swallowed the precious fire and jumped in. The hags jumped in behind him, then remembered they couldn't swim and jumped out again, screeching a great curse in their terrible voices.

At the opposite side of the lake Frog surfaced and hopped into the camp of the humans.

"But where is the fire?" they wailed.

Frog lurched forward and coughed a shower of sparks onto some dry kindling. The kindling smoked for a moment, then burst into flames.

The humans cheered Frog. They had fire at last. But Frog didn't cheer with them. In the chase he had lost his lovely tail. It never grew again.

To this day, tadpoles still wear their tails, but they cast them off when they are full grown as a mark of respect for their ancestor who helped bring fire to the humans.

## THE RAVEN AND THE WHALE

RIGHT from the beginning Raven thought he was more important than any of the humans or animals on his island. He would strut around with his chest flung out, lecturing everyone.

"Listen to me! Let me tell you what I think!"

The humans and animals all ignored him.

"Silly bird," they would laugh.

One day Raven flew into a tantrum. "I'm leaving this island," he screeched. "I'm moving to the mainland to make a name for myself."

Then he packed a bag of frozen fish for the journey and took off in the middle of a sleet storm.

Ice pellets pounded his feathers. Wild wind currents battered and buffeted him. After a while Raven couldn't figure out where the sky ended and the ocean began. He flapped his wings as hard as he could and flew around in circles. He was terrified and tiring quickly.

"Oh, no. This is it," groaned Raven.

He dropped down, down, but it wasn't until a large wave almost smacked him in the head that he realized he was about to plunge into the sea. He pulled up his feet sharply and in a great flurry of thrashing wings tried to avoid crashing into the icy water.

Just as his strength began to slip away, he noticed a dark shape looming out of the water.

"Ha! A rock," squawked Raven, and he hurtled himself at it. Seconds later he was swallowed up by darkness. He had flown into the mouth of a bow-headed whale.

He stared horrified into utter blackness. Then he panicked, and in the struggle to free himself, he became lodged deep in the whale's throat. He squirmed and twisted and squeezed and fell headfirst into a lighted room. A bright flame flickered from a stone oil lamp on a floor that was covered in furs. All around were walls made of soft hides. Across one end of this cozy den stretched a sleeping platform, and sitting on it with her legs tucked under her was a young woman whose beauty caused Raven to stare with his beak wide open.

"Welcome, stranger," said the young woman kindly to the soggy, bedraggled Raven.

Raven ruffled his feathers and thought, "What's all this?"

The young woman pointed to the hides on the sleeping platform. "Come, sit with me," she said.

When Raven had settled, the young woman rose and fetched baskets of mussels and crabs and delicious tiny fish.

Raven gulped down so much food that he fell into a deep sleep.

When he awoke he was alone. Suddenly the young woman reappeared with more fresh food.

Raven wanted the young woman to talk to him while he ate, but she kept jumping up and leaving, then returning and jumping up and leaving again.

Raven found this very annoying. He wanted all of her attention.

"Why do you keep jumping up and leaving?" he demanded irritably.

"I leave in order to live," she replied. "Breath is my life."

Raven was too interested in eating to pay attention to what she was telling him. He glared at her and started to argue.

"You don't have to leave. Stay and keep me company. I have important things to tell you."

But the young woman had no time to listen to Raven.

"I must go as soon as the need arises," she said firmly. "Furthermore, when I am out of the room, do not go near the lamp or try to touch it. If you disturb it in any way you will bring ill luck to all of us."

Then she disappeared again.

Raven frowned. "What is she talking about?" he thought.

For a few minutes, Raven was content to sit and digest his dinner.

"Hmm, nice place," he thought. "Warm bed, comfortable surroundings, good food, lovely girl. I deserve this."

As time passed, Raven grew fat, lazy and greedy. He took up as much room on the sleeping platform as he could. He talked only about himself and became very quarrelsome with the young woman. He even ordered her about as if she were his servant and this was his home.

One day while the young woman was out of the room, Raven felt particularly cross. He wanted to sleep but the lamp flame burned too brightly. In a moment of hotheadedness, Raven snatched the lamp and extinguished the flame.

Instantly he was plunged into darkness. There was a low rumbling quake and a shudder. The sides of the whale crashed in on him.

As he twisted this way and that through bone and blubber, Raven sobbed, "It's all her fault. She should have stayed with me."

Too late Raven realized that the bright flame had been the

spirit of the whale. The beautiful lady had been its soul which had to leave the den in order to breathe. Stupidly he had killed the spirit and soul of the whale.

The whale's body pitched helplessly from side to side on the surface of the water. Raven clawed his way out of the whale's broken body and perched on its head. His tail feathers had been torn off. One of his wings was broken, and most of the feathers had been ripped from his head.

Raven sat dazed and bleeding. Suddenly he stretched his neck. The whale was drifting toward his island. He could see the hunters paddling toward the whale in their kayaks to bring it ashore and harvest its meat and blubber. As the boats drew closer, Raven stood up, stretched his good wing and performed a little dance on the head of the whale.

"See," he squawked. "Did I not tell you what a great hunter I am? I alone have captured, killed and delivered this whale as a gift to you."

And the humans believed Raven. They stopped laughing at him. From that day on they looked up to him and celebrated him in their songs and stories.

# NOTES

THE REINDEER HERDER AND THE MOON
A retelling of a Chukchi fairy tale found in *A Mountain Of Gems: Fairy Tales of the Peoples of the Soviet Land*, translated by Irina Zheleznova. Moscow: Progress Publishers (English translation), 1975.

THE HONEST PENNY
A retelling of a Norwegian folktale found in *Tales From The Fjeld*, collected by P.C. Asbjornsen, translated by George W. Dasent. New York: Putnam's Sons, 1908.

KATYA AND THE GOAT WITH THE SILVER HOOF
A retelling of a legend of the Ural miners recorded by Pavel Bazhov in 1938 and found in *The Malachite Casket*, translated by Eve Manning. Moscow: Progress Publishers, 1981.

FROSTBITE
A retelling of a Lithuanian fairy tale found in *A Mountain of Gems: Fairy Tales of the Peoples of the Soviet Land*, translated by Irina Zheleznova. Moscow: Progress Publishers (English translation), 1975.

ANDERS' HAT
A retelling of a folktale from *Old Swedish Folk Tales* by Anna Wahlenberg, found in *For the Storyteller*, compiled by Carolyn Sherwin Bailey. Springfield, Massachusetts: Milton Bradley, 1920.

GOOD NEIGHBORS
A retelling of a Danish folktale found in *Yule-Tide Stories* by Benjamin Thorpe (ed.), London: Henry G. Bohn, 1853.

GRANDFATHER BEAR
A retelling of a folktale from Finland collected by Dr. James Cloyd Bowman, Margery Bianco and Aili Kolehmainen in *Tales From A Finnish Tupa*. Chicago: Albert Whitman and Co., 1936.

THE LITTLE GIRL WHO WANTED THE NORTHERN LIGHTS
Freely adapted from "The Stars in the Sky" found in *More English Fairy Tales*, collected by Joseph Jacobs. London: David Nutt, 1894.

HOW FROG HELPED PRAIRIE WOLF BRING FIRE TO THE HUMANS
A retelling of "Coyote [or] Prairie Wolf Brings Fire" found in *Snow Bird and the Water Tiger*, collected by Margaret Compton. London: Lawrence & Bullen, 1895.

THE RAVEN AND THE WHALE
A retelling based on variants found in:
"The Eskimo About Bering Strait" by Edward W. Nelson in *Eighteenth Annual Report of the Bureau of American Ethnology for the Years 1896-1897*, J.W. Powell, Director. Washington: Government Printing Office, 1899.

*The Eagle's Gift: Alaska Eskimo Tales* by Knud Rasmussen, translated by Isobel Hutchinson. Garden City, New Jersey: Doubleday, Doron, 1932.

*Elik and Other Stories of the Mackenzie Eskimos*, collected by Herbert Schwartz. Toronto: McClelland & Stewart, 1970.

*The Eskimo Storyteller: Folktales from Noatak, Alaska*, compiled by Edwin S. Hull, Jr. Knoxville: University of Tennessee Press, 1975.

My thanks to the staff of the Osborne Collection, Toronto Public Library, for helping me to locate needed sources.